Special thanks to Michael Ford

ORCHARD BOOKS

First published in Great Britain in 2018 by The Watts Publishing Group

1 3 5 7 9 10 8 6 4 2

Text © 2018 Beast Quest Limited
Cover and inside illustrations by Dynamo
© Beast Quest Limited 2018

Team Hero is a registered trademark in the European Union
Series created by Beast Quest Limited, London

A CIP catalogue record for this book is available from the British Library.

ISBN 978 1 40835 201 4

Printed in Great Britain

MIX
Paper from
responsible sources
FSC® C104740

The paper and board used in this book are made from wood from responsible sources.

Orchard Books
An imprint of Hachette Children's Group
Part of The Watts Publishing Group Limited
Carmelite House, 50 Victoria Embankment, London EC4Y 0DZ

An Hachette UK Company
www.hachette.co.uk
www.hachettechildrens.co.uk

REVENGE OF THE DRAGON

ADAM BLADE

ORCHARD

MEET *TEAM HERO* ...

JACK

POWER: Super-strength

LIKES: Ventura City FC

DISLIKES: Bullies

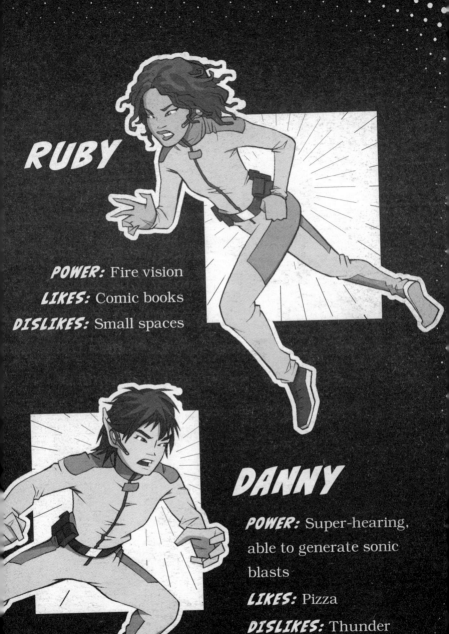

RUBY

POWER: Fire vision

LIKES: Comic books

DISLIKES: Small spaces

DANNY

POWER: Super-hearing, able to generate sonic blasts

LIKES: Pizza

DISLIKES: Thunder

CONTENTS

PROLOGUE   9

EXPELLED!   17

AN OLD FRIEND?   37

CAMOUFLAGE   55

RAINA'S CHARGE   75

TERROR TRANSFORMATION   95

BELLY OF THE BEAST   111

"RAINA," PLEADED Olly through parched lips. "Help me ..."

He writhed in the rusted manacles that kept him spreadeagled against the stone wall of the cell.

How dare the Legion do this to me? When I get out I'll scorch them all to ashes!

The thought brought a smile to his

cruel face, and he felt power surge
through the Flameguard. The magical
breastplate could blast beams of
white-hot fire at his enemies. The
fools had tried to take it from him
several times, but it wouldn't budge.
*Of course not! It's part of
me now.* Sadly, for the moment,
they'd wrapped him in a steel
straitjacket as well, so he couldn't
use the weapon, but soon ...

He'd start with the student who
brought him slops to eat.

*How long have I been down here?
Five days? When am I getting out?*

The Flameguard tingled, and then

Raina's hissing voice came from all around. It seeped from the walls.

"Your patient wait is over," she said. "It is time to take the final step on our journey together."

"What journey?" said Olly moodily. "I've been chained to a wall for days!"

"An enemy is most vulnerable when he is most confident," said Raina. "Commandant Eckles and your former allies of Team Hero think they are winning, but my powers are almost fully returned. I have one of the Orbs of Foresight, my magical smoke-steed Porphus, and now the Inferno Sceptre. There is only one more artefact I require, and you will help me claim it."

"That's more like it!" said Olly. "Have you got a key for these manacles?"

"Keys are for mere mortals," said Raina. "As my power grows, so does your own! Can't you feel it?"

Olly felt the Flameguard grow warm. New strength crept through his muscles.

"I do!" he said. "It's ... magnificent!"

"Then *use* it," said Raina fiercely. "Seize control!"

Olly roared, flexing the tendons of his arms and legs. The chains that bound him cracked apart, falling in heavy chunks to the floor of the cell. Olly fell forward but managed to land on his feet. He ripped off the straitjacket too and the cell filled with a red light as the veins of fire across the Flameguard's surface glowed like trails of lava.

As the light spread into the shadows, Olly saw a cloaked figure lurking in the far corner. *Raina! Has she been here all along?* He couldn't see her face under her hood, and he wasn't sure he wanted to.

"What now?" he said.

Raina drifted towards him, feet floating across the stone floor, until she stood right at his side. Now she was closer, Olly noticed that she flickered slightly like flames and he could see the stone wall of the cell through her body. *She's not really*

here. It's just a magical image. The
projection of Raina whispered her
plan into his ear, and as she did, he
grinned. He turned to her, about to
reply, but she was gone.

Olly faced the cell door, spread
his arms and let the power of the
Flameguard gather across his chest.
The trails of fire came together at the
centre, growing red, then orange, then
yellow, then white. A beam of pure
energy shot forth, and turned the
door to liquid metal in an instant.

*Imagine what it could do to my
enemies!* thought Olly gleefully.

CHAPTER 1

EXPELLED!

"I THINK I've made myself clear," snapped Eckles. "You are expelled!"

"But we were sent here to help the Legion defeat Raina," said Jack. "She's still out there."

Eckles's face twitched. "We can handle Raina quite effectively without you," she said.

She can't really believe that, thought Jack. *Without us, many of the Legion would have died already.*

"If I could say something ..." Danny began. He looked to be in pain. Jack guessed his bat-like super-sensitive ears weren't appreciating the volume of Eckles's telling-off.

"No, you may not," said Eckles. "I'm sending word to Chancellor Rex at Hero Academy that you'll be returning at once."

She turned her back on them and marched away, armour clanking as she descended a set of stairs.

Ruby turned to Jack, her bright

orange eyes aglow with desperation. "What now?"

"I really don't know," he replied quietly.

He thought of Chancellor Rex and how disappointed he'd be. The headmaster wanted Team Hero and the Legion to be allies, but after this incident, that seemed unlikely. *We've really messed things up this time.*

It had all happened because they'd simply told the truth — that all the evidence pointed to the possibility that Wulfstan Hightower, founder of the Legion, and General Gore were one and the same. Jack wasn't sure exactly why or how the legendary hero had become one of their deadliest enemies, but items they'd discovered in Wulfstan's secret chamber under the archive room left them in little doubt.

"Well, I for one am looking forward to Hero Academy food again," said Danny brightly. "If I have to eat one more mouthful of that mutton stew ..."

He went quiet as both Jack and Ruby glared at him.

"Just saying — clouds, silver linings ..." he muttered.

They were traipsing towards the stairs when Fronn emerged from another, smaller wooden door. The young Legion sage was dressed in his trailing scholar's robes, with his arms folded in front of him, hands hidden in his baggy sleeves.

"We do not have much time," he whispered. He withdrew his hands and Jack saw a small, rolled-up scroll. "On further investigation of the secret chamber of Wulfstan's you uncovered, I found this. I am not entirely sure of its meaning."

Jack took the scroll from him and unravelled it.

"I believe the sketch was made by Wulfstan himself," added Fronn.

Jack's friends crowded closer to

look as well. The image was faded by time, but quite clearly showed the sorceress Raina's head and body. The yellow eyes were unmistakable — but a dragon's wings extended where her arms should be, and a long, whipping tail flexed in place of her legs.

"Why is she breathing smoke?" asked Danny.

"Eckles said she was part dragon," said Ruby. "Dragons breathe fire, so some smoke makes sense."

"But I don't think it's smoke," said Fronn warily.

Jack's blood ran cold as he stared at the billowing clouds of darkness coming from Raina's mouth.

"It's Noxxian shadow," he muttered.

"But that's impossible!" said Ruby. "Raina isn't from Noxx. Only creatures of that realm can control the shadow."

They all turned at the sound of

footsteps on the stairs. Jack rolled the scroll quickly, tucking it away up his sleeve. Three armed Legionaries entered the room, including Lieutenant Derik, the second-in-command at the outpost under Lieutenant Stark.

"We have orders to escort you off Legion territory," he said. From the deep blush of shame on his cheeks, Jack realised he was carrying out his orders unwillingly. It was hardly surprising, as they'd fought Raina side by side while helping save the town of Bernshoff.

"Yes, of course," said Jack.

As he turned to leave, he felt Fronn

press something into his hand. He looked down. Three black stones glittered in his palm. *Shadow gems.*

"I found these in the chamber as well," whispered Fronn.

Jack frowned. It was their discovery of a similar gem that made them realise Wulfstan had become General Gore. There was no other reason the founder of the Legion should have had such dangerous artefacts from the dark realm of Noxx. If the gems broke, they'd release deadly shadow. Jack was immune, but his friends were not. Danny had suffered the shadow's corruption in the past, and

it had almost
cost him his
life. Jack
vowed he
would find a
safe place to
dispose of the
gems at Hero

Academy, far away from Legion lands.

● ● ●

Soon they were marching down the
dusty hillside, out of the Shardmaw
Mountain passes. At the head of the
party, Derik rode Flinta the accifax,
who was half lion and half eagle.
Her feathered head was dipped, and

occasionally she let out a miserable squawk, as if she too was sad that Jack and his friends were leaving. Jack patted her tawny furred flank to comfort her. *We went through some adventures together ...*

He, Ruby and Danny were on foot, with the other two escorts at the rear. One of the guards was carrying Danny's energy crossbow, Ruby's mirror shield and Jack's sunsteel sword, Blaze. They had orders from Commandant Eckles to return them only when they reached the borders of the Legion's territory. It was a pointless gesture, thought Jack. She couldn't take their *real* weapons, the gifts that had brought them all to the Hero Academy — Jack's scaled, super-strong hands, Ruby's fire-beam eyes, and Danny's ability to release sonic booms from his throat.

"I hope you understand, I'd rather not be doing this," said Derik, as they stopped by a river for the accifax to drink. "For what it's worth, I think Eckles is wrong to send you away."

"Don't worry about it," said Jack kindly. He'd grown rather fond of the gruff lieutenant.

"Someone's coming," said Danny suddenly, his ears twitching.

Flinta lifted her dripping beak from the water, and the Legionaries all drew their swords.

But the figure that approached around the bend was a young woman clutching a baby. And behind her came other desperate-looking villagers carrying bundles of clothing on their backs, some with faces smudged with soot. They called out when they saw Jack's party, throwing themselves to their knees and begging for help.

"Are you all right, young lady? What's happened?" asked Derik.

The woman with the baby was

weeping. "Our village! It's been burned to the ground."

"I'm so sorry," Jack said. "Who attacked you?" he asked, though he already feared the answer.

"A terrible gang of hellish creatures," rasped an elderly man, his clothes ash-streaked and ragged. "They had the heads of bulls

and the bodies of men ... but they were made of flame, like glowing embers from the hearth-fire. So many were killed ..."

"Raina's horned warriors!" gasped Ruby in horror.

"Some of them must have somehow survived the flood in the Cinderfall valley," added Danny.

"Please," said the young woman, "for my child's sake, let us take shelter behind the thick walls of Mount Razor. If they come back, we would not survive another attack."

Derik looked uncertain for a moment, but then nodded grimly. "Alfren," he said to one of the other Legionaries, "escort these people to the fortress. Make sure they're given food and medical attention, and find them beds in the dormitories."

"Thank you!" came the chorus. Jack watched as Alfren led the people up the path towards Mount Razor.

I hope they're safe, he thought. *Though if Raina attacks, I fear even the walls of Mount Razor won't be enough to protect them.*

They continued on their journey with just two escorts, and as they rounded the head of the valley, Jack saw the torched remains of the village that spanned a small river. Collapsed buildings still smoked and dead livestock lay strewn across the track.

Raina will do the same to Mount Razor if she gets the chance …

"Please, let us return and talk to Eckles," said Jack. 'She needs all the fighters she can muster."

"I wish I could," said Derik, staring sadly at the desolation. "But her mind is made—"

A fierce snort cut him off, and from behind a heap of debris stepped the colossal figure of an ember warrior. His horns spread three feet across, and flames jetted from his nostrils.

Fire dripped from the double-headed axe in his grip.

Derik drew his sword and spurred Flinta on with a battle cry. Raina's servant stood his ground, and began to swing his axe in arcs around his head.

"For the Legion!" roared Derik.

His sword met the axe in a shower of sparks, but the foe was too powerful. Jack looked on in horror as the force of the parry lifted Derik from the saddle and hurled him face-first into the rocky riverbank. He lay in the shallow water, groaning in pain. The remaining Legionary dropped the mirrored shield, crossbow and Blaze, then sprinted away as fast as his armoured legs would carry him. Jack and his friends each picked up their weapons.

"I guess it's up to us," said Jack.

CHAPTER 2

AN OLD FRIEND?

THE HORNED warrior charged, lifting his axe. Flinta reared and snorted in panic.

"I'll handle this!" said Ruby. She dropped into a crouch, and her eyes glowed bright with fire. Twin beams shot forth, blasting the axe from their enemy's hands. He lowered his head and ran on regardless, horns-first. Danny let rip a sonic blast, and it smashed into the warrior's chest, lifting him off his feet and dumping him on the ground. Ruby went to help Derik, while Danny managed to grab Flinta's reins.

Jack leapt forward with Blaze and placed the point against the ember soldier's neck.

"You've lost," he said. "The villagers are safe, and we're taking you back to Mount Razor."

The foul beast cackled, and his voice was like sifting ashes. "Mount Razor cannot protect you," he said.

"When Raina strikes, it will crumble, with all of the Legion inside it."

Suddenly the warrior kicked out, catching Jack in the stomach. He folded in two, helpless, as the creature grabbed his axe once more and hefted it over his head, ready to cleave Jack's skull in two.

A blade burst from the horned warrior's chest, and it froze, mouth open in astonishment, before collapsing into cinders and chunks of charred bone at Jack's feet. Derik stood behind it, sword in one hand. He dropped the blade, and cradled his other arm.

"Thank you!" said Jack.

"The least I could do," the Legionary replied.

"You've hurt your arm," said Ruby.

"I think it's broken," muttered Derik. "No matter. Do you really think Raina would dare to strike at Mount Razor itself?"

"I think we've underestimated her from the start," said Jack.

Derik's face was grave. "Take Flinta.

I can't ride like this. I'll walk back to Fort Stonetree and warn them."

"Does this mean we're not expelled any more?" asked Danny.

Derik arched an eyebrow. "That's for Commandant Eckles to decide, but if you were to steal Flinta and ride back, I could hardly stop you." He smiled grimly.

The three of them climbed up on to the accifax.

"Good luck," said Derik.

Jack nodded and dug his heels into Flinta's flanks, and the huge creature launched itself up the path, back the way they'd come.

I only hope we're not too late ...

• • •

Before long, the looming battlements of the school rose into view. From a distance, Mount Razor looked impregnable, but Raina was devious, and growing more powerful by the day. Jack had to remind himself that she'd used her shape-shifting ability to gain access to the school once before, pretending to be a teacher called Captain Jana. It would take more than high walls of thick stone to keep her out.

"Even if we get there in time," said Ruby darkly, "we don't actually know if we'll be able to defeat Raina."

"As long as we get the students to safety, that's a start," said Jack, but he knew that might be easier said than done. Raina wouldn't give up until the entire Legion was destroyed. She wanted nothing more than revenge for her defeat at their hands a thousand years ago. Besides, before they could even begin preparations for defending the fortress, they had to convince Commandant Eckles that the threat was real.

Flinta seemed to sense their urgency, and ate up the rocky path in huge strides. As her paws thudded down, Jack's teeth rattled in his head and he gripped the reins with his scaled hands.

A shadow flitted overhead, and Jack's first thought was that it must be a mountain eagle. But then a figure descended until it hovered over the path in front of them, and he reined Flinta to a halt. Jack's eyes focused on the gleaming metal of the breastplate, flowing with red rivulets like blood. *The Flameguard.* His eyes travelled up until they landed on a familiar sneer.

Olly!

"Oh, great!" said Danny. "Just when

I thought things couldn't get any worse."

"How did you get out?" asked Jack. The last time he'd seen his former fellow Hero Academy

student, he'd been locked in the bowels of Mount Razor in a dank and dingy jail cell. And it was no less than the traitor deserved.

Olly, his face sweating and smeared with dirt, laughed. "You really think Raina would let her most trusted ally rot in a cell?"

"Er … yes?" said Ruby. "You've been there for quite a few days, haven't you?"

Olly's face darkened. "It was all part of our plan!" he said in a slightly whiny voice. "Lull our enemies into a false sense of security, then strike when the time is right! If I were you, Heroes, I'd turn and scurry away like the rats you are."

"Nice try," said Danny. "But we're not going anywhere."

Jack drew Blaze as he and his friends slid off Flinta's saddle. "And you're going right back into that cell."

"Let's see about that, shall we?" said Olly.

Ruby blasted her streams of fire, and Jack flinched from the heat that seared past his head. But Olly didn't even move. He spread his arms as the flames hit his chest. To  Jack's horror, the breastplate seemed simply to absorb them, glowing brighter than before.

"Ever heard the expression 'you can't fight fire with fire'?" said Olly. His eyes flashed. "My turn!"

Three beams of energy burst from his chest, right towards each of them.

Jack shoved his friends one way and dived the other. When he looked back, three puddles of molten rock bubbled where they'd been standing. Flinta snorted and backed away.

Danny roared, and Jack saw the air ripple in a shockwave. The sonic blast rippled the skin of Olly's face, but he held his position, even inching forwards, until Danny sagged back, his energy spent.

"How ... ?" gasped Ruby.

"I told you, I fight for Raina now," said Olly. "Ever since we joined together, I've felt invincible. You losers picked the wrong side!"

Jack pretended to be groggy as he stood up, staggering to his feet. "You two — try and keep him distracted," he whispered.

Danny ran one way, retreating behind a boulder with his crossbow, while Ruby blasted more fire as she sprinted beneath Olly. For a moment, he seemed confused, unsure which way to look. A bolt from Danny's crossbow clattered into Olly's

Flameguard, bouncing off, and Ruby's
fire-beam hit him in the back. While
Olly was occupied, Jack vaulted
on to Flinta, kicking the accifax
into a gallop up a steep slope that
overlooked the clearing where Olly
was hovering. Olly was still distracted
by Ruby and Danny's flames and
energy bolts when Jack charged
Flinta on to a rocky overhang ten
metres from Olly's position.

I've got to time this right ...

Just as Olly returned fire at Ruby
and Danny, his own beam of energy
cutting swathes of smoke through
the landscape, Jack hurled himself

through the air. His momentum carried him in an arc, limbs wheeling towards his enemy from above.

At the last moment, Jack grabbed Olly around the chest, and they tumbled through the air in a knot of limbs. Olly righted himself, just before they hit the ground. "Get your lizard hands off me!" he roared.

"'Fraid not!" said Jack.

He squeezed as hard as he could, hoping to make Olly give in. But the older boy growled, and under his hands, Jack felt a sudden surge of heat from the Flameguard.

"You'll burn to a crisp!" sneered Olly.

Jack gritted his teeth and held on, but the heat became unbearable, and in the end he had to let go. He fell to the ground, landing with a thud that buckled his knees and knocked the breath from his lungs.

Whatever Raina's done to Olly has made him unstoppable!

With Jack unable to get his breath and stand, Olly focused his attention on Ruby and Danny. They were both sheltering behind a car-sized boulder, but as Olly's energy blast hit the rock, it began to glow, first red, then orange. Before Jack's eyes, it started to melt like an ice cube.

Jack's friends had nowhere left to run.

CHAPTER 3

CAMOUFLAGE

"YOU'RE TEAM Hero, Olly!" roared Jack. "You don't have to do this!"

But the manic look in Olly's eyes told a different story. *He's Raina's servant now. He won't stop until he's killed us all.*

Ruby and Danny huddled close. Flinta had returned to Jack's side.

I know she wants to help, but what could she do?

Jack's hands were glowing, but with Olly high in the air, there was no chance of reaching him.

Jack's eyes fell on a rock the size of an apple. *Perfect!* He dropped quickly, grabbed the stone and hurled it. The missile glanced off Olly's head,

spinning him
in the air.
He rolled,
clutching
his head and
howling in
pain.

Ruby and Danny rushed towards Jack but as the smoke cleared, there was no sign of Olly.

"He'll be back," Jack said bitterly.

"I don't get it," said Ruby. "Olly was always a bully, but he's turned properly demonic!"

Still, despite everything, Jack felt sorry for Olly. He was Raina's slave now, and it was partly Olly's jealousy for Jack that had led him along that path. If anything happened to Olly, Jack would feel terrible. "Let's get to Mount Razor before he shows up again," he said to his friends.

Danny turned towards the distant

school. "Kestrel, give me a zoom, please," he said to his Oracle. A visor extended over his eyes from the earpiece. "Could be tricky," he said. "Take a look."

The other two summoned their own Oracles, and when Jack focused on the walls of Mount Razor he saw what Danny meant. The perimeter defences were teeming with guards clutching crossbows, as well as giant catapults and slingshots ready to hurl boulders at anyone foolish enough to approach uninvited.

But none of those weapons can stop Raina, thought Jack.

"At least Eckles is taking the threat seriously," said Ruby.

"Problem is, she won't hesitate to use that artillery against us!" said Danny grimly.

"We'd have to be invisible to sneak past all those guards," Jack said. "If we just ride up on Flinta, we'll be killed in seconds."

Danny clicked his fingers. "That's it! We need to be invisible."

The other two looked at him like he was mad. "Great plan!" said Jack. "I'll grab my invisibility cloak. Oh wait. There's no such thing."

"Very funny," said Danny. "Don't

you remember?" he added, gesturing around. "This is near where we first met the jotun — the rock giant."

"*Met?*" said Ruby. "You mean when it tried to squish us."

"That was just a misunderstanding," said Danny. "I tried to blast it with my sonic power because I thought it was just any old rock."

Jack caught on. "Yes! Because it was *camouflaged*," he said. "So if we can summon the jotun again, we can use it to sneak up on Mount Razor unseen."

"It's one of my better plans, right?" said Danny.

"Small problem," said Ruby. "The Legion summon jotun with a special mountain horn. We don't have one."

Danny looked crestfallen, but Jack wasn't ready to give up.

"We have the next best thing. Hawk, have you got an audio file for a Legion mountain horn?"

His Oracle spoke calmly in his ear. *"I have over three billion individual sound files, from a baby crying for its rattle to a tree falling in the forest on a rainy morning."*

"Just the horn will do," said Jack, grinning. "Maximum volume through external speaker, please."

The valley filled suddenly with the low, mournful sound of a horn. Jack stared around, turning on the spot, but no jotun appeared.

"It was worth a try," said Ruby. "I guess we'll just have to ... whoa!"

The ground a metre or two away began to rumble, and then rocks shifted of their own accord, stacking on top of one another as the shape of a gigantic figure unfolded from the ground. Where before there'd been just a collection of boulders, now there stood a walking giant, three metres tall. Patches of his body were covered in lichen, and his head was a boulder the size of a small car, with a gash for a mouth and two hollows for eyes.

"Er ... hi!" said Danny.

"Who wake?" asked the jotun. His body made a grinding sound as his joints shifted.

"Us!" said Ruby. "Down here!"

The jotun's massive head bent. "You no smell like Legion. You no talk like Legion. Me crush you. Make you flat. Then me sleep."

Jack stepped in front of his friends. "No! Listen, please! The Legion are in grave danger and we are the only ones who can help."

The jotun was still for a moment. "No squish?" he said.

"No squish!" said Danny. "Help us!"

The jotun seemed to shrug. "Then me sleep?"

"Yes!" said Ruby.

The creature seemed to think about it, then nodded its rocky head.

Jack was relieved. He hadn't much fancied trying to fight a stone giant after everything else that had happened that day.

"Help us to get to Mount Razor — unseen," he said.

The jotun twisted his body, and Jack saw huge crevices in his back, wide

enough for them to sit. "Me carry,"
said the jotun.

Jack had to put his doubts aside,

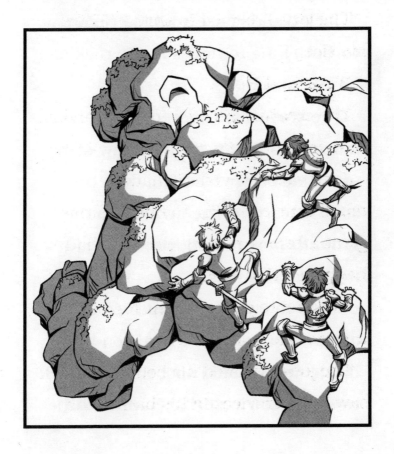

and they climbed on to the creature's back together. "Hold on," said the jotun, as it straightened up.

Jack couldn't see a lot to grip on to, but clung to ridges in the rock as best he could.

The stone giant moved with surprising agility, taking a few steps at a time before blending with the rock faces, or crouching low to the ground. Jack peered through a crack in the jotun's frame, using Hawk to scan the walls. He expected that at any moment, the guards on the battlements would spot them and raise the alarm. If that happened, he really didn't have a plan B.

"Take it slowly!" he whispered to the jotun, as it leapt ten metres in a single bound. A guard peered down, seemingly right at them, but then kept walking.

"Admit it — this was an outstanding idea," said Danny.

"Let's save the celebrations until we're in," Ruby replied.

At the base of the fortress wall, the jotun began to climb, reaching up with massive fingers and gripping the uneven stone. Hand over hand, they rose in juddering steps. Jack tried not to look down. A fall from here, and

they'd be doing Raina's job for her.

They were almost at the top when

Jack heard a crunch above, and the

jotun's hand slipped back. Showers of rock fell past, plummeting far below, and a guard came rushing along the defences. The jotun flattened himself against the fortress and froze.

The guard stared, less than fifty paces away on the wall, but he couldn't see them.

"What's the matter?" called another guard, joining the first.

"Thought I saw something," said the guard, blinking.

"You're being paranoid," said his friend. "Nothing there but rocks."

The first guard squinted for a few seconds more, then continued his patrol. Jack hadn't realised he was holding his breath until it all came out in a rush. *That was too close*.

When the coast was clear, the jotun climbed a few more metres, then Jack and the others hopped off his back and on to the walkway that circled the fortress walls.

"The Legion thanks you," he said to the jotun, who bobbed his head in return before turning to leave.

Without waiting a moment more, the three friends sneaked through the nearest door and into the labyrinthine corridors of Mount Razor. The fortress was in chaos, with students and soldiers running this way and that, gathering weapons and armour. Since Jack and his friends were dressed in Legion garb, no one paid them the slightest attention as they made their way down a staircase towards the main chamber. Before they even reached it, Jack heard panicked voices.

"We're telling you, they flattened our whole village. Raina is coming!"

"What are we supposed to do now?"

"The Legion are supposed to protect us, aren't they?"

They reached an archway and peered into the torchlit hall.

Commandant Eckles was surrounded by soldiers, and in front of her were the villagers from earlier that day, plus Alfren, the escort who had returned with them.

Eckles lifted her hands for silence, and gradually the room quietened. "You are completely safe here," she said. "The walls of this fortress have never been breached."

"Have you even seen her warriors?" asked the lead villager. "You don't know what you're up against!"

The shouting began again. Eckles tried to calm them, but she couldn't.

Jack had heard enough. Without

waiting for his friends, he strode into the chamber. The villagers parted, letting him pass, and the Legionaries beside Eckles stared, gobsmacked. Jack's friends hurried after him.

Commandant Eckles was the last to notice their presence, and her face darkened at their approach.

"Commandant," said Jack. "These people are right. Unless we act now — together — Mount Razor will fall."

"Arrest them!" said Eckles.

The Legionaries spread out. In no time at all, Jack and his friends were encircled, and outnumbered, with sword points at their chests.

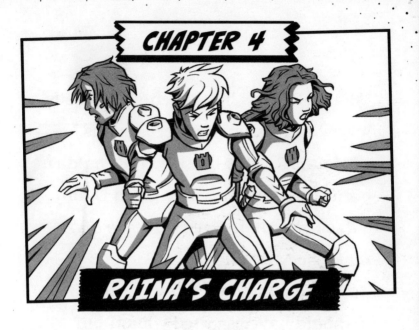

CHAPTER 4

RAINA'S CHARGE

JACK ALMOST drew his sword, but held back. Ruby kept her fire-beams in check, and Danny made no attempt to string one of his crossbow bolts.

"Can't you see we're not your enemy?" said Jack. "We are on the same side. Let us help you now."

"We do not need help!" roared Eckles.

"Mount Razor's battlements can easily withstand Raina and her minions."

"Mount Razor's battlements couldn't even withstand us three," said Danny.

Jack shot him a glare. *Please don't make her any angrier!*

The Commandant's jaw tightened. "I should have escorted you off our territory myself!"

"Commandant!" A red-faced Legionary student burst through the door. It was Matthias, Mount Razor's head boy. "Word from the scouts!"

"What is it?" snapped Eckles.

"S-something's coming towards Mount Razor," said Matthias.

Commandant Eckles pointed at the cowering villagers. "All of you, stay here. Legionaries — to the walls."

"What about us?" asked Jack.

"Don't move!" said Eckles. "I'll deal with you later."

She led the soldiers from the chamber, her face grim.

"That went well," said Danny, glancing at his friends.

"Are we really going to stay out of it?" asked Ruby.

"No way!" said Jack. "Eckles needs us — even if she doesn't realise it yet!"

They ran after the soldiers, making their way towards the outer battlements. In the distance, coming over the crest of a nearby range, was a cloud of rising dust. Jack asked Hawk to magnify the scene, and the sight confirmed his worst fears. It wasn't dust at all — it was black smoke rising from the galloping hooves of Porphus the shadow stallion. His horned head lowered and jets of blue flame snorted from his flared nostrils. Once he had been a peaceful creature, dwelling in the volcanic caves, but Raina had corrupted him. The sorceress rode on Porphus's back, cloak billowing and gaze centred on the walls of Mount Razor.

The whole valley seemed to quake with the stamping of Porphus's hooves, and Jack saw the knees of some of the younger archers were knocking. *All the training, all the drills ... nothing could have prepared them for this.*

A single archer loosed an arrow that fizzed harmlessly towards the ground.

"Hold fire!" bellowed Eckles. "Wait for my order."

All eyes were fixed on the approaching figure, growing larger by the second as it ate up the ground quicker than any racehorse. Then, through the smoke that surrounded

Raina, another figure appeared. Jack didn't need Hawk's zoom function to tell him who it was. The bright red breastplate gave it away. That, and the fact he was airborne, several metres above the ground.

"I knew we hadn't seen the last of Olly!" sighed Danny.

"Ready, archers!" yelled Eckles, and the soldiers braced themselves. Jack saw Raina dig her heels into Porphus's flanks.

"Nock!" shouted Eckles. The archers placed arrows to bowstrings.

"Draw!" They pulled back the bowstrings, arrows pointing skyward.

Raina was three hundred metres out and closing. She galloped across open ground, not even attempting to stay under cover. Jack dared to hope their enemy had miscalculated.

"*FIRE!*"

Countless shafts cut through the sky, rising in a high arc over the rocky plain below. As one, they began to dip in a deadly hail of sharpened metal points.

Only one has to find its target, thought Jack.

Olly puffed out his chest, and the Flameguard sent out dozens of rays of energy. Each caught a shaft mid-flight, incinerating it into flakes of falling ash. Not a single arrow made it through, and Jack heard the gasp of shock reverberating through the ranks of soldiers on the walls. Eckles's face was pale.

"Again!" she cried. "Nock ... Draw ..." The soldiers obeyed her commands in perfect time. "Fire!"

The sweep of shafts rose and fell once more, but again Olly's breastplate wiped out the wave of arrows in a single blast. Porphus kept coming, carrying his mistress, and Olly stayed right above them.

"Trebuchets!" yelled Eckles. "Catapults! Everything we've got!"

Soldiers scurried like ants over the assault weapons, loading rocks or flaming pitch into the leather slings. Legionaries cranked the mechanisms into life, and wood creaked as chains rattled over pulleys, adding tension. Jack found he was holding his breath.

"Fire at will!" cried Eckles. Rocks and fire whistled out across the approach, a terrifying volley of artillery. Olly blasted some aside, but Raina changed direction too, as the rocks smashed into the ground on either side. Porphus leapt over a rolling fireball with a whinny of alarm, as smoke and dust enveloped everything below. Suddenly the clatter of hooves died, and there was no sound at all.

"We did it!" a voice rang out in triumph. "We got them!"

Cheers started to spread along the

fortifications, and whoops of relief and joy. Jack was almost swept up in the euphoria, but then a gust of wind tickled his fringe. Below, the smoke cleared suddenly, whipped aside. And there, perhaps two hundred metres from the walls, stood Porphus, ghostly black flanks rising and falling. On his back Raina lifted the Inferno Sceptre, the orb at its head glowing red.

"Is that all you've got?" she shouted. "This will be easier than I expected!"

She thrust out the sceptre and a fireball coursed from its tip, slamming into one of the trebuchets. Jack heard screams of terror, and saw Legionaries

falling from the battlements to the ground below. Another fireball smashed into the wall near Eckles, throwing out rocks and sparks and flames. Though the Commandant held her ground, Jack could see from her bewildered face that she had no idea what to do next.

Raina launched a third orb of fire, which spun into one of Mount Razor's upper towers. Stone crunched and cracked, and the whole tower tipped perilously.

"Excellent!" said Olly, floating down to her side. "Which bit shall I shoot?"

Raina reached out and touched his shoulder. Through his visor's zoom function, Jack saw an odd look in her eye as she stared at Olly — cunning, and full of hate. He knew in a heartbeat that something bad was about to happen.

"Olly — look out!" he yelled.

Raina's hand gripped the back of Olly's neck, making him fold up in pain, and dragged him down towards her.

"Hey! What are you doing?" he cried.

Raina's face was alive with evil. "You've served your purpose, slave."

"I thought we were partners!" said Olly. He wriggled like a fish on a hook, hands scrabbling at hers to try to break free.

"I'm afraid I work alone!" said Raina. "Time for me to reclaim the final artefact."

"No!" said Olly. "It's connected to me! It hurts! Please ... no .... Argghhh!"

The shriek that left his lips made

Jack shudder as Raina ripped the Flameguard from Olly, and then dropped him to the ground like a rag doll. Olly lay still, curled into a ball.

The final artefact? "It was the Flameguard all along!" said Jack.

Raina had dismounted from Porphus, and one of the Orbs of Foresight shone from her eye socket. She lifted the Flameguard over her head, and Jack saw it magically clamp over her, fitting her slender form perfectly.

Across the battlements, soldiers stared, dumbstruck, while others had already begun to retreat. Raina lifted the Inferno Sceptre, and black clouds rolled across the sky, lightning flashing through their undersides.

"I feel it!" yelled Raina, her voice like the boom of thunder. "After so long, I feel all of my power return."

A blinding fork of lightning sliced down, touching the sceptre's tip. Jack shielded his eyes. Even then, the afterburn of the strike left kaleidoscopic colours behind his eyelids. When he looked again, Raina was on her knees. "Is she hurt?" asked Ruby hopefully.

"I don't think so," muttered Jack. Raina was *changing*.

Her body thrashed and pulsed under her robes. The back of her cloak tore open, and two great leathery wings sprouted forth and flexed. As she lifted her head, one eye glowed milky white, the other yellow. The Flameguard had morphed into some sort of second skin of black scales that completely covered her torso. Jack remembered the image on Wulfstan's scroll, of a creature half woman, half dragon. And as a thick scaly tail whipped around from where Raina's legs had been, he realised the transformation was complete.

"Behold my true form," she cried,

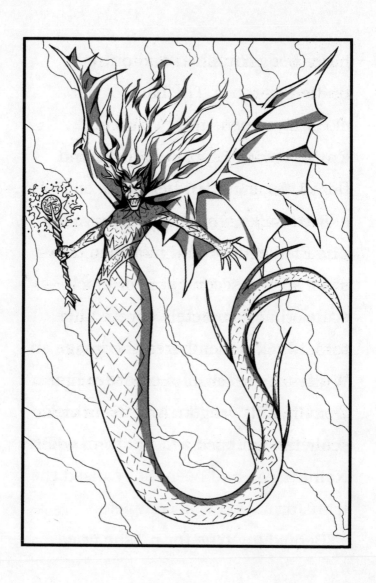

her voice carrying easily to the battlements.

"Hold your ground!" bellowed Commandant Eckles. "She cannot take Mount Razor!"

With two mighty flaps, Raina rose powerfully into the air, leaving Olly's inert body, and Porphus, on the plain.

"I won't be taking anything," she said, her black hair streaming free. "I will crush Mount Razor to dust! You thought your little fortress could protect you, but it will be your tomb!"

CHAPTER 5

TERROR TRANSFORMATION

RAINA FLEW up, her dragon tail swaying sinuously behind her.

"Commandant!" shouted Jack. "You have to evacuate the fortress! Everyone left inside will be killed."

"Nonsense!" replied Eckles. "These walls have stood for a thousand years. It'll take more than a few—"

Whooosh!

Raina launched a spinning white fireball from the Inferno Sceptre into one of the tallest towers above.

Jack looked on in horror as stonework began to rain down, then the tower itself broke loose, toppling in what seemed like slow motion.

"You were saying?" said Danny.

Eckles was trembling in her armour. "Everyone — back to the inner walls!"

The Legionaries hurried through any door they could find, away from the perimeter wall and into the bowels of Mount Razor.

"That's no solution!" said Ruby.

"They'll be buried alive."

Raina swooped low, launching more fireballs at the base of the mountain. Each one struck home, showering fragments of rock and leaving fortifications quaking.

As Jack reached for Blaze, his hand brushed something in his pocket. The three shadow gems. With all the commotion, he'd completely forgotten they were there. And as he touched them, he couldn't help but think back to that strange image on Wulfstan's scroll again. He'd thought it made no sense that Raina was breathing shadow, and perhaps that's because she wasn't. He remembered the vision he'd had through the Orb of Foresight of Wulfstan defeating Raina, before he'd turned evil. What if the shadow was actually destroying her? Maybe Wulfstan had drawn the moment of her defeat!

"Guys, I've got a plan!" he called to the others.

"Does it involve desperate heroism in the face of almost certain death?" asked Danny.

"You read my mind," said Jack, managing a smile. He took out one of the gems. "I think Wulfstan kept these for a reason — to vanquish

Raina in case she ever returned."

Ruby peered down at the dragon-woman. "Good luck trying to get anywhere near her."

"We need to make her come to us," said Jack.

"I know just the thing," said a voice. They all turned to see Matthias, the young Legionary, his face streaked with ash.

"All the others have run away," said

Danny. "Maybe you should too."

Matthias scowled. "I'm not letting Team Hero take all the credit!" he said. "Come on — follow me!"

"Where to?" asked Ruby.

Matthias pointed at Raina. "She's missing an eye, isn't she? I bet she'd kill for the other Orb of Foresight."

"I think she'd kill for just about any reason, actually," Danny said.

"But it's still a good idea!" said Jack. "Let's get it!"

They plunged back into the corridor with Matthias. Torches guttered on the walls as the assault continued below. Cracks were snaking across stone floors and stairways. Finally they reached the treasury, but the doors were locked.

"Allow me!" said Jack. His hands shone gold, and he punched the doors right off their hinges.

"Eckles won't be happy when she sees that," muttered Danny.

"The whole fortress is about to be demolished," said Ruby. "A broken door or two is the least of her worries."

Jack grabbed the second Orb of Foresight from its plinth. The ancient object could cause distracting visions of the past and future if touched directly, so he handled it with a piece of cloth he'd found nearby. "We need to get to the roof," he said.

They found a narrow staircase and hurried up in single file until they reached the very top set of battlements, near to the crumbled tower Raina had destroyed. From on high, the full extent of the destruction was clear. Fires were burning across the fortress below, and several sections of wall had already collapsed or looked close to giving way. Raina hurled the fireballs relentlessly, taking the revenge she'd been plotting for ten centuries.

She hasn't a drop of mercy in her.

She won't stop until the entire Legion is massacred.

Jack handed the Noxxian gems to Danny. "Fix these to your arrows," he said. "I'll draw Raina in with the Orb, and you fire when she's close."

"What about you?" said Ruby.

"I'll be fine. If she gets too close, give her a blast of fire," said Jack.

Ruby looked uncertain at first, but nodded. "Good luck, Jack," she said.

Jack walked out across the battlements and lifted the Orb high over his head. "Hey, Raina! I think you're missing something!"

The sorceress tilted her head and

focused on him. For a moment, he feared she wouldn't come, but then her wings pumped, carrying her higher, and right towards him. *She won't blast me with fire and risk destroying the other Orb ... I hope ...*

As the dragon woman rose to face Jack, Danny was crouched behind a wall out of sight, with the gem fixed to the shaft of an arrow.

"Give that to me!" Raina shrieked.

Come closer ...

"If I do, will you spare Mount Razor?" Jack asked, biding his time.

"It's too late for that," she snarled. "But I will make sure you die quickly."

Jack shrugged, pretending to mull it over. "And if I don't?"

"Then I'll tear you limb from limb," said Raina. She tucked her wings and swooped towards him at top speed.

"Now!" he shouted.

Danny shot the arrow, and Jack heard a pop as the gem exploded across Raina's dragon hide. But at the same time she rose away, leaving the cloud of shadow hanging uselessly in the air.

"A trick! I should have guessed," she hissed. "Want to try again?"

Danny had already reloaded and loosed a second arrow. Raina twisted in the air and the arrow flew past, missing its target.

Danny threw a desperate glance at Jack, and his thoughts were clear enough. *Only one gem left. We can't afford to waste it.*

"Time to watch your bat-eared friend die," said Raina, lifting the Inferno Sceptre.

"Danny, look out!" cried Jack.

But there was nowhere for Danny to run as the fireball streaked towards him. At the last moment, Ruby hurled herself from her vantage point and landed in front of Danny, holding up her mirror shield. The impact of

Raina's attack knocked Ruby down into Danny, while her shield sent the fireball ricocheting like a comet straight back at Raina. It smashed into the villain's scaled chest, sending her spinning through the air.

Danny peered out from behind Ruby. "Take it!" he called, and lobbed the final gem to Jack. He snatched it from the air and slipped it into his pocket, just as Raina reappeared.

"You shouldn't have made me cross, little heroes," she said.

And she began to change once more, her scales blackening. It took Jack a few seconds to understand what was happening, as her skull lengthened into a muzzle. Then her arms stiffened and curled into stubby clawed legs.

She's shape-shifting! She's becoming full dragon!

Her eyes were the only clue that the creature was still Raina.

Spreading her wings on the thermal currents rising from below, she breathed a snort of black smoke and

fixed her gaze on Jack.

No weapon could stop such a colossal beast.

But maybe that's the answer!

Jack formed a plan quickly. A mad plan that would almost certainly kill him. But if it worked, it would be the end of Raina too.

CHAPTER 6

BELLY OF THE BEAST

JACK SPREAD his arms wide, the Orb glowing in his hand.

The enormous dragon folded its wings and dived towards him. Jack stood his ground.

"Jack, get out of the way!" came the cry from Ruby below.

"Run!" yelled Danny.

Jack stared into the dragon's jaws, wide enough to swallow him whole.

Or so he hoped.

Raina's eyes — one yellow, one white — fixed on his, and he saw triumph in her deranged gaze.

Jack hurled himself into her open throat. He saw the flash of teeth, and then he was tumbling through the wet slime of her gullet. Dim light from the Orb showed the red tissues of her insides, and he felt the thump of her heart all around him. Jack's fingers clasped the last shadow gem.

Got you, he thought, and crushed it in his hands.

Shadow exploded all around him, seeping into Raina's flesh, and Jack heard her shriek of pain vibrate through her body. It felt like he was being jolted back and forth until a sudden, tremendous force seemed to grip him by the feet and drag him back up the dragon's throat. He was thrown out of the creature's jaws. Rocky ground rushed towards his face.

Thump!

His body crumpled up. After a moment, he opened his eyes to see a rubble-strewn courtyard.

Dizzy, he saw four figures rushing towards him. Then they became two, and he realised it was his friends.

As they helped him up, a howling cry filled the air. The dragon was writhing in the sky, shadow pouring from her nostrils, her mouth, even her eyes.

Scales flaked from her body, scattering like fallen leaves, then the Orb of Foresight fell from her eye socket like a stone, exploding into fragments as it hit the ground. Jack saw, through the cloud of shadow, an almost human face, mouth gaping in despair, and a hand clutching the Inferno Sceptre. Then the weapon too cracked apart, dissolving into ash.

The remains of the dragon crashed into a wall, before sliding to the bottom in a heap of dust and shadow. Jack and his friends edged closer, their weapons ready to face whatever emerged from the debris. But when

Jack saw what remained, he held up his hand to stop them.

Raina was crouched against the wall. She looked similar to when they'd first met her. An ancient crone in tattered robes, her spindly arms raised in terror. Her pale, blind eyes were wide.

"Please, don't hurt me," she begged.

Jack sheathed his sword, filled with pity. They had won.

Mount Razor was safe once more.

● ● ●

Two days later, Jack and his friends stood before the gates of the Legionary school. The fortress walls were scorched, and several sections had crumbled away, but the magnificent structure was still standing. While last time they had left under armed guard, the circumstances couldn't be more different now. Legionaries in gleaming armour formed two lines threading away from the gates.

"I was wrong," said Eckles. "Mount Razor would be nothing but rubble if it weren't for your bravery."

Jack bowed respectfully. "Raina was more powerful than anyone imagined," he replied.

The Commandant blushed. "No. You knew and you tried to tell me, but I was too stubborn and arrogant to listen. At

Mount Razor, we have looked inwardly for too long, shunning the help of our old friends, but from this day forth that will change. Team Hero and the Legion will be allies again."

"I'm glad to hear it!" said Danny.

"Don't forget, we had help," said Ruby. "Fronn, Derik, the jotun, Matthias ..."

"And Flinta!" said Jack.

The accifax, emblazoned in decorative armour herself, let out a squawk.

Eckles laughed, for the very first time Jack could recall.

"I will be sending commendations to Chancellor Rex," she said. "You are all a credit to his school."

Not all of us, thought Jack grimly. He glanced back to the fortress, his mood dipping.

"How is Olly?" he asked.

Fronn shook his head gravely. "He has regained consciousness," he said, "but it will be a long road to recovery. Both his body and mind have suffered great damage."

"I never thought I'd say this," said Danny, "but I hope Rex goes easy on him. It wasn't entirely his fault. The Flameguard corrupted his mind."

They saluted Commandant Eckles, who saluted back.

"Safe travels, Team Hero," she said.

On the walls above, a sentry blew a horn, and the columns of Legionaries lifted their lances to form an arch. As Jack and his friends passed underneath, many nodded or smiled

from behind their helmets.

"Perhaps one day we'll come again," said Ruby, beaming with pride.

"I hope so," said Jack. *I'll never forget the lessons I learnt here.*

When they reached the end of the lines, the foothills of the Shardmaw Mountains stretching out before them, Jack saw a shape come over a crest ahead. For a second, his heart tightened, until he realised what it was.

"Porphus!" cried Danny, breaking into a run.

The graceful white stallion cantered towards him, trailing wisps of pure steam. As they came together, the horse lowered his head and nuzzled at Danny's shoulder.

"I think Danny will miss this place too," muttered Ruby. "He's got a soft spot for that horse."

Danny turned around. "I don't know what you're talking about," he said, his eyes gleaming as Porphus galloped away towards his cavern near the Summer Sea. "I'm just looking forward to getting back to the Academy. Do you think they'll throw us a party?"

"Chancellor Rex isn't the partying sort," said Ruby.

Jack laughed. "Maybe we'll just get some extra rations."

"I suppose that will have to do," said Danny glumly. "At least no one will be trying to kill us for a while."

As the three of them marched away from Mount Razor, Jack wondered how long the peace would last. If there was one thing life had taught him since he began at Hero Academy, it was that evil lurked where you least expected it.

But Team Hero will always be ready.

IN EVERY BOOK OF
TEAM HERO SERIES
ONE there is a special
Power Token. Collect
all four tokens to get
an exclusive Team Hero
Club pack. The pack
contains everything you and
your friends need to form your
very own Team Hero Club.

MEMBERSHIP CARDS • MEMBERSHIP CERTIFICATE • STICKERS • POWER GAME • BOOKMARKS

Just fill in the form below, send it in with your four tokens
and we'll send you your Team Hero Club Pack.

SEND TO: Team Hero Club Pack Offer, Hachette Children's Books,
Marketing Department, Carmelite House, 50 Victoria Embankment,
London, EC4Y 0DZ.

CLOSING DATE: 31st December 2018

WWW.TEAMHEROBOOKS.CO.UK

Please complete using capital letters *(UK and Republic of Ireland residents only)*

FIRST NAME
SURNAME
DATE OF BIRTH
ADDRESS LINE 1
ADDRESS LINE 2
ADDRESS LINE 3
POSTCODE
PARENT OR GUARDIAN'S EMAIL

I'd like to receive Team Hero email newsletters and information about
other great Hachette Children's Group offers (I can unsubscribe at any time)

Terms and conditions apply. For full terms and conditions please go to
teamherobooks.co.uk/terms

TEAM HERO Club packs
available while stocks last.
Terms and conditions apply.

COLLECT ALL OF SERIES THREE!